The Copper Braid of Shannon O'Shea

LAURA ESCKELSON

• ◦ • ◦ •

illustrated by
PAM NEWTON

DUTTON CHILDREN'S BOOKS • ◦ • ◦ • NEW YORK

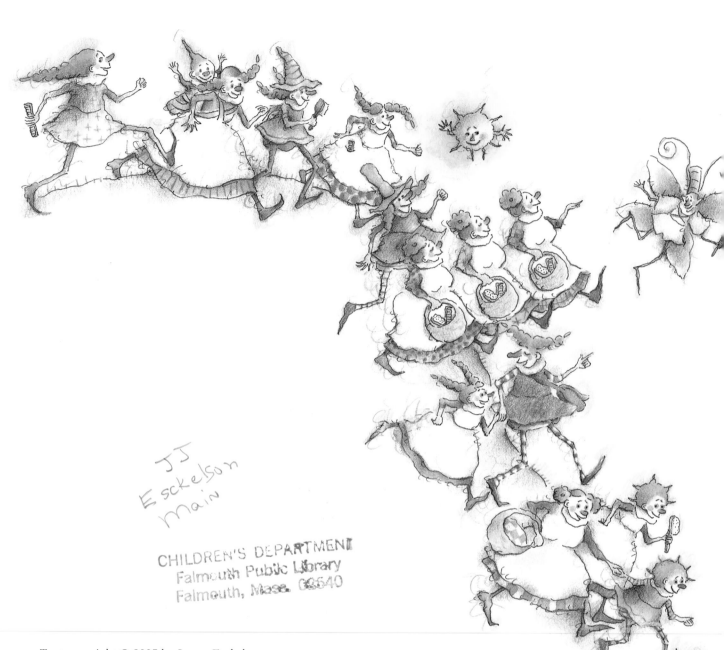

Text copyright © 2003 by Laura Eskelson
Illustrations copyright © 2003 by Pam Newton
All rights reserved.

CIP Data is available.

Published in the United States 2003
by Dutton Children's Books,
a division of Penguin Putnam Books for Young Readers
345 Hudson Street, New York, New York 10014
www.penguinputnam.com

Designed by Alyssa Morris and Irene Vandervoort
Manufactured in China
First Edition
ISBN 0-525-46138-8
10 9 8 7 6 5 4 3 2 1

*For my mom, with thanks for reading
to me when I was young* —L.E.

*For Dr. George Martin, M.D., who
stops my sneezes, and for Anna
Colozzo, who cuts my hair!* —P.N.

The copper braid of Shannon O'Shea
Was unbraided one fall on account of the hay
Which had tangled into the plaits of her hair,
But nobody knew what else snarled in there.

It started quite simply, with one golden piece
Plucked from the locks by the wily Bernice,
A queen among sprites who envied the way
Light shimmered around the stray wisp of hay.

The sprites should have known to leave the braid bound,
To not start unknotting and fooling around
When new bits of hay seemed to sprout from her hair
Until she was sneezing with each breath of air.

They began to unfasten her ribbons and bows,
Finding thimbles of silver quite jumbled in those.
There were buttons of metal and buttons of glass,
Buttons so small they could button the grass.

Then they stumbled on crab apples tucked in the braid,
And a dusty old jar of orange marmalade.
Bernice found raccoons and a rather large crow,
Nibbling on corn in a dark copper row.

The pollen and dust unloosed from the hay
Kept Shannon sneezing all through the day.
But nobody heard the sound of her sneeze,
Completely drowned out by the honking of geese.

The geese had been flying south for the fall
When a strand of her hair had captured them all,
Along with some seagulls in search of the ocean,
Squawking and making a giant commotion.

They unraveled, untangled, unlooped as they pruned
Twigs from her hair and silky cocoons
Of butterflies, moths, and a flock of lost loons
Who thought they were in a copper lagoon.

As they unbraided, a song filled the air
From some carolers who had been tangled in there,
And when they were found, were puzzled to find
The holidays over and nine months behind.

Her unbraided hair twisted in gyres,
Spun into steeples and pillars and spires.
The sprites were bedazzled and charmed by her hair.
Each uncoiled knot seemed to whirl in the air.

The busy unbraiders found purple potatoes
And fried them along with some wild green tomatoes,
And when they had finished the last of their feast,
They discovered a glen full of marvelous beasts.

A griffin curled up with a silvery lynx
And a hummingbird perched on the head of a sphinx,
All gathered upon a carpet together,
Woven from whisker and cobweb and feather.

Then they found emeralds and nuggets of gold,
Combed from the soil and held in a fold
Of the bright copper hair curved like a crown
That glowed in the sky when the sun had gone down.

Limos and taxis rolled out with a sputter,
With Mary Jo Tucker's churn for her butter
And the old barn cat, come to no harm,
Along with the cows from the Hendersons' farm,

Thought to have vanished in last year's flood.
They came out unfazed and chewing their cud,
After a frantic stampede through the air
Released them at last from the locks of her hair.

The sprites were amazed when they found a small boat
Adrift in the waves of a coppery moat.
They found a green goblet and named it the Grail,
And a single red herring caught by the tail.

Hair curled around clouds as it tumbled undone,
And the sky became dark as it covered the sun.
The sprites used lanterns and coal miners' hats
To discover a way to get out of all that.

They found a volcano where wildflowers grew,
Meadowlarks, mice, and a shy kangaroo,
A dinosaur egg, a blue praying mantis,
And a small island which they named Atlantis.

Because they'd been working day after day,
They thought they'd grown closer to Shannon O'Shea,
But when they called out for the copper-haired girl,
They became more entwined in the maze of her curls.

When they tried to turn back, they felt just as lost.
The hair that they'd combed recoiled and recrossed.
So they went on ahead with no end in sight
And silently labored by day and by night.

They followed the strands of the coppery hair
And were gently removing a bear sleeping there,
Curled in the shade of a small grove of trees,
When all of a sudden, they heard a loud sneeze.

And just at that moment, they all reached the girl
And remembered the hay in the coppery curl
Plucked from the braid by the wily Bernice,
Who envied the brilliance of one golden piece.

When they were done with all the unbraiding,
They began reeling and wild serenading,
And Shannon joined in with the laughter and song
After she'd asked them, "What took you so long?"

It took dozens of sprites to rebraid the hair
Of Shannon O'Shea, who sat on a chair
Seventeen miles from the end of her braid,
Quietly sipping an iced lemonade.

Now all who come to the village are told
What was found, one fall, in the coppery fold
Of young Shannon's braid, the bright shining stream,
Where sometimes a tangle is more than it seems.

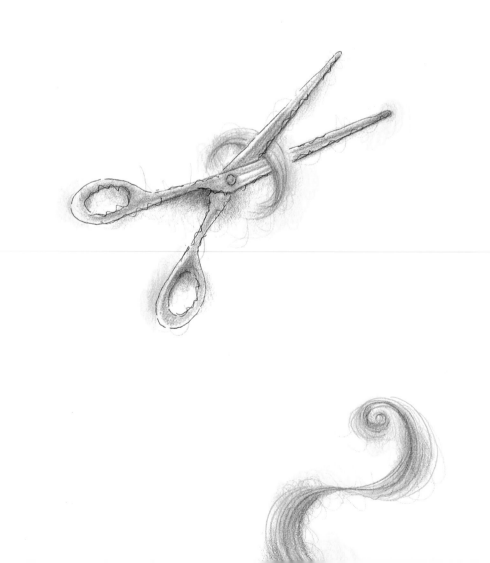